SIT ME DOWN

A M/M CHAIR ROMANCE

ROOM MATES
BOOK 2

SABRINA CROSS

AUTHOR'S NOTE

This is a sentient object romance. Humans will be getting it on with sentient objects. Don't worry, everyone is gleefully consenting.

If you read the last three sentences and think that's not for you, that's okay. There is still time to put this book down and walk away. No one will blame you. It's the sane thing to do.

But if you're going to stick around please be aware of the following: Overbearing parent, financial manipulation, animal death from hunting (off page), voyeurism, chair humping, woman scared to death (off page), dubcon, ugly purple chair, depictions of anxiety, alcohol use, sex with a chair, dirty shirts, face fucking.

If you feel I am missing anything please reach out to me at authorsabrinacross@gmail.com and let me know. A complete list can be found at www.sabrinacross.com

1 EVAN

"That is the ugliest chair I've ever seen," my roommate, Dave, says as he walks into the living room. He drops into an ancient brown recliner roughly the color of dried shit. I turn my attention back to arranging my new find to face toward the TV.

"It's not that bad." It's kind of that bad. The chair is bright purple with black legs. It's that old-fashioned type of chair my grandmother had a bunch of. Though hers were blue and green and not gaudy purple.

"No one will have to question your sexuality again. They just have to ask who the chair belongs to and they'll know." I shoot him the bird and drop down into the chair. It's ugly, but comfy as fuck.

The seat is soft and squishy, the back is high and supports my head and neck. The fabric is some sort of soft fuzzy material. But classy. In a gaudy way. It really is fucking ugly.

"One word: free."

"Nice." Dave leans forward and grabs the video game controllers from the beat coffee table that has seen better days. He tosses one to me and powers up the system. "Still fucking ugly."

I don't argue because he's not wrong. Beggars can't be choosers.

We'd had a nice set up. Until our buddy Jake moved out a couple weeks ago with his boyfriend, who showed up out of nowhere. He'd taken all of his furniture with him, the bastard. I mean, good for him for finding happiness or whatever, but I miss his couch.

There was a time where I wouldn't have had to worry about money. I would have mentioned to Dad we needed a couch and boom, one would be delivered a few days later. But things with Dad have been shit since I decided to go for my master's degree. Mom convinced him to let me keep the off-campus house they'd bought for my siblings and I, but everything else is up to me.

Bye-bye included utilities. Sayonara grocery delivery. Peace out monthly allowance. Hello part-time jobs and budgeting. Nice to meet you online marketplace and thrift stores. This year has been humbling, to say the least. But it's worth it to finally be doing what I want to do, rather than what Dad says is best for me.

I don't want to be like my siblings who gave up their lives to fit the mold he shoves them into. They all work for the family business, went to the school he chose, date the people he approves of. I'll never be that person, and I'm tired of trying.

"You've gotta get that chair out of here before tonight, man. We'll be mocked for the rest of the year." I glare at my oldest friend and remaining roommate. He's not wrong. The chair, no matter how comfortable it is, isn't the vibe.

"I'll take it to my room."

"Cool. Let's keep looking for a couch."

2 EVAN

stumble into my bedroom and close the door behind me. I try to flip the lock but miss and decide fuck it. A little more stumbling and I'm in my comfy, ugly chair. The room is spinning as I struggle to get my high-tops off. I'm almost tempted to say fuck it and sleep with them on. But no, I don't want to do the laundry.

Finally, I get the knots free and shoes off. I lean against the high back of the chair and sigh. I am way too drunk. Stupid, stupid drunk. At least I removed myself from the party before I made yet another bad decision.

Well, mostly.

I'd stopped making out with Austin, the star of the school hockey team, before I let it go any further. Again.

I have a rule against closeted men for a reason and Austin isn't about to come out of the closet any time soon. I'd let him turn me into his dirty little secret but I was over it. Done. So what if the man sucked cock like a hoover?

A man has to have a little dignity, right?

Arousal and alcohol hum through me as I take in the slightly woodsy scent of the chair. I could go back downstairs and try to find someone to fuck. But the risk of me ending up back in bed with Austin is too high. Why does he have to be so pretty?

Instead, I fumble through opening my jeans. I shove them and my boxers down far enough to kick them off before wrapping a hand around my dick. I tilt my head back and close my eyes, willing the spinning sensation to stop so I can focus on the firm grip on my cock.

The woodsy smell of the chair increases as I pump my hand up and down a few times, trying to find the right rhythm. It gets into my head and I imagine someone else's hand on my dick. He'd be large and a little hard, his hands callused. I shudder as I imagine the rough texture moving against me.

Would he be willing to suck me off? Or would he demand I bend over and take what he has to give me? I whimper at the possibilities. Fuck, I need to get laid.

My hips buck as I stroke myself but it isn't enough. I need something. Something else. Something more.

I hit the arm of the chair with my elbow and grunt. Then freeze.

No, I couldn't.

It's deranged. Totally unhinged.

And yet.

I move before I can fully think it through and talk myself out of it. The room tilts a little as I swing over the arm of the chair and plant my foot on the floor. My left hand grips the back while I press my right hand to the top of my dick.

The material offers a soft friction as I begin to move against the piece of purple furniture. I bend forward until my face is nearly pressed against the wing, until I'm drowning in that woodsy scent.

3 DRAKE

Existence is a funny thing.

One moment you're a messenger to the gods, going about your life. And the next moment you're a fucking chair. I'll take some blame in my downfall. I had wandered out of the safety of the Otherworld and onto the human plane. Something I knew better than to do.

But still, the indignity of my situation is intolerable. I'd tried asking for help from my previous owner. It had ended poorly. I'd shocked the elderly woman to death.

Poor luck, that.

For a time, I worried I would end up in the dump. The children of the woman I'd scared to death hadn't wanted me around. Can't say I blame them. Dead lady chair is a tough sell.

Still, it was a relief when I'd been picked up by a young guy and taken to his house. Even better when I was moved from the living room to his bedroom. Now I had a chance to speak to him in private and plead my case.

Fucking humbling to have to beg a human for help. The boy barely looks old enough to shave. But he's the only hope I have of ever returning to my old life. Chairs can't summon goddesses, apparently.

Unless she is punishing me for straying onto the human plane. It would be just like a goddess to ignore my cries for help out of spite.

I'm choosing to believe the former. I cannot be stuck like this forever. The thought is intolerable.

The door to the room opens and loud music pours inside. I internally cringe at the sound and am thankful when the door closes quickly and it's muffled again. The humans are having a party. I'm not entirely positive what that means on the human plane, but it sounds terrible and cacophonous.

Stumbling footsteps come at me from behind and then the human who brought me home comes into view. He flops down onto me and I stifle back an oomph at the sudden, unexpected weight of him. Don't want to startle him.

For a moment, I think about the odd magic keeping me alive in this chair prison. I can see and hear, even move a little bit. But I have no eyes or ears. I have no mouth to speak, but that doesn't stop me from being able to make sound. It's strange and hurts my head if I think about it too hard.

Thankfully, horrifyingly, the human gives me something to think about. He's removed his shoes and now is undoing his pants. He tugs them down and kicks them aside before taking himself in hand.

I try not to be a voyeur. I do my best to focus my attention elsewhere as he pumps his cock in his fist. I think about the Otherworld. About my goddess and her home there. About the joys and misery of my position in the Pantheon.

Anything, oh anything, but the sight and sounds of the attractive man stroking himself.

But then he has to go and do it. He shifts and turns until his weight is resting against the arm of the chair, which feels strangely like my leg in sensation. And he begins to move.

His cock is pressed between my limb and his hand, giving us both friction. He leans forward and buries his face against the wing of my chair and it's like I can feel his breath on my neck. And then he's moving, grinding and humping against me.

It's depraved. It's unhinged. It may be the hottest thing that's ever happened to me in centuries of existence.

4 EVAN

The chair tips a bit as I thrust against it. I've worked my way up the arm until the tip of my cock presses against the winged edge with every thrust. Electricity runs down my spine as my balls draw up.

I'm close. So fucking close.

The woodsy smell is everywhere. The chair almost feels like it's vibrating beneath me. I groan as I move faster. Faster, faster.

And, with one final thrust against the back, I come. I collapse against the chair as I try to catch my breath. My leg braced on the ground shakes beneath me.

"I do hope you're planning on cleaning that up." A deep voice says. I jerk up and look toward the door, but it's still closed.

"What the fuck?" I say, scrambling to my feet to find the source of the voice. I drop a hand to cover my junk as I search for my boxers on the floor. My cock is still hard and covered in cum. The nice afterglow of orgasm gone before I even got to enjoy it.

Thankfully, the worst of the drunk seems to be gone too. Unless that's why I'm hearing voices. Could just be the alcohol talking.

"The copious amount of fluid coating my fabric. I assume you're going to clean it up."

Yeah, definitely the alcohol talking. Because I know for certain my chair isn't talking to me. I've seen some weird shit in my time, but I'm not crazy enough to believe that.

Assured that I'm alone, I head into the master bath to grab a damp cloth to clean my cock. And yes, the chair. I'll have to grab some cleaner tomorrow. When the house isn't filled with people to ask questions about why I needed it.

I cannot believe I just fucked my chair. What the fuck is wrong with me?

After wiping down my dick, I toss the cloth into the hamper and grab another one. I get it damp and squirt some hand soap onto the square before heading back into the bedroom. I can hear the music pumping through the door and am just sober enough to wish that they would all go home.

Embarrassment floods through me as I approach the gaudy purple seat. What was I thinking? Nothing good, clearly.

I begin wiping down the velvety fabric. Scrubbing away the evidence of my moment of horny insanity.

"Gentle, fuck."

I jump back and drop the cloth as the deep voice comes again. "Are you trying to rub me raw?"

I shake my head, trying to clear it. I'm hearing things. That's all. I'll go to sleep and wake up in the morning and this will all be something to laugh at.

Except how the fuck am I supposed to sleep with a talking chair in my room?

I'm not. I won't. So I do the only thing I can do.

I shove the chair into the hallway and lock the door behind me.

5 DRAKE

Well, this is an unfortunate turn of events.

I lean back against the wall and sigh. At least this one didn't die of fright. Though he doesn't seem to believe that I'm real. That's a problem.

How does one convince as human of the supernatural when everything they're told from birth insists it doesn't exist? I don't have any answers but I have to find them. And soon.

Before the human decides to get rid of me. Or worse. Didn't college students like to burn furniture? I feel like that's a thing. And it isn't a thing I want any part of. Shooting me didn't end in my death, but fire almost certainly would.

At some point, a girl stumbles her way up the stairs and curls up on my seat. Another man brings a man and a woman upstairs to an adjoining room. The trio pays me and my occupant no mind.

Maybe blackmail would work. Fucking furniture isn't a normal behavior and it's possible the human would do anything to avoid knowledge of that act getting out. But who would listen? The drunken girl drooling on my arm?

No, I must appeal to him somehow. Convince him he wants to help me. If only I had any idea of how to do that.

The night goes on, the trio leaves and the dark-haired boy returns on his own. The girl sleeps on, completely unaware. And the door behind me doesn't open again.

It isn't until light floods through the window at the end of the hall that the door opens again. The human is there, dressed in a pair of loose jeans and a tight white t-shirt. He stops beside me but my hope is dashed when his focus is entirely on the girl still sleeping upon my seat.

I watch as he gently wakes her and gets her to her feet and down the stairs. He's capable of softness and sensitivity. I can use that to my advantage.

Eventually, the other boy exits his room and goes downstairs. I wait, but no one returns.

Fine, I'll take matters into my own hands. With great focus and effort, I begin to move. The human left the door slightly ajar and I force my way through the opening and back into his bedroom.

He can't ignore me forever. And next time, I'll make him pay attention.

6 EVAN

The chair is back in the middle of my room when I get home from class and work. I kick myself for not telling Dave to leave it where it was.

Not that I could explain why I didn't want the thing in my room. Not really.

"Sorry Dave, can't have the chair in my room. It talks." I say aloud, rolling my eyes at myself even as I give the chair a wide berth on my way to the bed.

"At least you're admitting it," the deep voice from last night says.

I jump and spin around.

"I was afraid you'd convince yourself I was just a drunken hallucination and we'd have to start all over again."

The chair shifts and I stumble back a step and land on my bed. My bag falls off my shoulder and lands on the floor with a loud thump. I ignore it as the chair continues to shift from side to side in front of me.

"What the fuck?"

"Listen, I get it. This is weird. Let's move past all of the freaking out and get on with it." The voice is deep and smooth. It seems to be going for soothing but is more snark than anything.

"I think I'll stick with the panic, thanks." I draw my legs up onto the bed as the chair slides forward across the wood floor. It bumps against the bed and I bite back a yelp.

"This is impossible." I say, hugging my legs to my chest.

"Nothing is impossible." The chair says. Because yeah, I'm pretty sure it's the chair doing the talking. "Well, a few things are, I suppose. But not nearly as many things as you humans think."

There's a beat of silence while I try to process that statement. It's a chair, so it's obviously not human. But chairs don't talk, so it's obviously not just a chair. What am I dealing with here?

The way I see it, I have two options. Either my chair is talking to me or I've completely lost my mind and am hallucinating. I'm pretty sure I'm not crazy, so talking chair it is.

"What are you?" I ask, trying to release my grip on my legs but my muscles aren't obeying. Panic fills every cell of my body.

"I am a messenger for the goddess Brigid," the chair shifts back a little bit and I'm finally able to release my death grip on my legs. "And I need your help."

7 EVAN

"Right, yeah, of course." Because a chair messenger to a goddess makes total sense. Maybe the chair flies and carries the goddess wherever she needs to go.

"Oh, for fuck's sake." The chair practically sags onto itself with the sigh it releases. It's a whole body thing that for some reason calms me. "I wasn't always a chair. So whatever nonsense you just spun in your head, forget it."

The fact that the chair knew what I was thinking was more than a little concerning. Maybe the chair could read minds. Could it manipulate them? Is that why I did...what I did the night before? It makes more sense than me randomly deciding to hump a chair.

"Are you in my head? What did you do to me?" The words were more panicked than the demand I'd been going for.

"I didn't do anything to you. Your thoughts are written on your face." The chair tilts to the side and then lets out a deep laugh. "If anyone violated anyone here..."

Heat rushes to my face. I think about what I did,

the absolutely unhinged behavior of fucking a chair.

"Don't worry about it," the chair says. "It was hot. In all my years, I've never been ridden quite like that. Though, I do usually like to know the name of the person fucking me."

"Evan," I say automatically, before I can even consider it.

"Evan," the chair repeats. He drawls it out in that deep voice and it stirs something in me. Something that shouldn't be stirring over a fucking chair. "I'm Drake."

I snort. A chair named Drake is as absurd as a talking chair. The whole thing is absurd. Absolutely ridiculous.

"I wasn't always a chair, you know." The chair leans forward, wood creaking. Springs, squeaking. "Once, I had many forms. This is my prison. My hell."

8 DRAKE

"How does one become a chair? Piss off a god?" Evan's question is sarcastic, but his body has begun to relax as we've talked so I answer it anyway. If I can get him relaxed enough to hear me out, maybe he will help me.

"Oh, I'm sure my goddess is pissed. But she's not the reason I'm stuck in this form." I sigh and settle back into myself. "Brigid's messengers take the form of the goose. We're given flight and safe passage through the pantheons and otherworld. Don't kill the messenger isn't just a human phrase but a theological promise among our kind."

I sigh, thinking of my stupidity. "Unfortunately, humans aren't among our kind and aren't bound to our rules. I was on my way back to Brigid's territory when I wandered off the path and into the human plane. Hunters found me and I was shot."

"You didn't die." It wasn't a question, but the question was there.

"We cannot be killed by human weapons. Our spirits are more than our physical forms. So when I was shot and my feathers plucked for this chair, my spirit stayed with them. I am trapped here without means of escape."

"That sucks." The words are flippant but the sympathy is sincere. "What does that have to do with me?"

"I cannot summon the goddess in my form. She may not know where I am, or she may be punishing me for my mistake. Either way, I need a human to summon her so she may restore me."

Evan laughed, a mirthless sound. "I don't know how to summon a goddess."

"I can help you." I lean forward again, all of my focus and intent on the human. "Please, you're my only hope."

I don't mention the old lady I'd scared to death. Or the possibility of him passing me onto someone else who wouldn't believe me. I don't let myself think about being thrown into the trash left to rot for centuries among the garbage. Or worse, burned and snuffed out of existence entirely. No, I need this human to summon Brigid and save me.

And I know he can save me. I don't know why, but I'm absolutely certain this human is going to be my salvation. I can feel it deep down in my soul, we are kismet.

"Then I guess we're summoning a goddess."

The thing about summoning a goddess, they often ignore the call. The summoning is easy. Most humans include trappings and symbolism to the act but really, it's all about the intent. One doesn't need to cast a circle, candles and sacrifices. They only need to focus and beg for assistance.

The problem is, deities spend every moment of every day receiving requests. In the past, they tried to answer some of them. But these days, they mostly just ignore them all. Without the power of human worship, entering the human plane isn't as easy as it once was. And they don't feel the need to respond to the human's calls.

I'd hoped that Evan's request would be different enough to catch Brigid's attention. I was clearly mistaken.

"I'm sorry," Evan says, climbing to his feet after long moments of prayer. "I don't feel anything."

"Trying is all I can ask." Resignation settles into my soul as I come to terms with the fact I am never escaping this form.

9 EVAN

There's something wrong with my chair. Drake has been calm, subdued. I don't know how I know that this isn't normal for him, but it feels wrong.

I mean, I get it. I'd be pretty pissy if I was stuck as a chair for all of eternity too. It's been a week since I tried summoning his goddess without success and he's been growing more and more withdrawn since then.

As weird as it is, I like having him around. It's kind of nice to know I have someone to come home to after a long day at school and work. Dave and I have conflicting schedules most days and don't get to spend much time together anymore. Jake's stopped by once since he moved in with his boyfriend Lux, but they're so into each other it's like no one else is in the room when they're together.

We really need to fill Jake's old room, but Dave and I haven't found anyone who doesn't give off serial killer or 'I collect my toenails in a jar' vibes. We're getting by without the rent money, so we have time to be choosy.

So yeah, it's nice having someone around when I get home. Someone to talk to in the few hours after work before I'm finally able to fall asleep. And Drake specifically, isn't bad to have there.

His voice, deep and lilting, does it for me in a way I'd never admit out loud. The woodsy smell of the chair now permeates every corner of my room. Which is nice, but also a problem because it still turns me on in a way I've ever experienced before.

I've been jerking it in the shower twice a day just to survive. And I still wake up hard and ready to go every morning. Something Drake either doesn't notice or is kind enough not to call out.

It's Saturday night. Dave went out with some friends but I opted to stay home. The bar scene has been getting dull for a while and I couldn't bear the thought of that many people in the house again.

And honestly, I just want some alone time with my chair. He has interesting stories and tales of the gods. It was like a mythology class come to life. And okay, maybe it was better than any mythology class I'd ever taken because it was all being told to me in that deep, lightly accented voice.

"How's it going?" I ask, not really sure how to get him to open up and talk to me. But I realize I really want him to.

"Just fine."

It is the least sincere fine I'd ever heard in my life. The kind of fine you tell someone who asks you how it's going and you know they don't want to hear the truth. The kind of fine you tell someone when you want to spare them your messy feelings or don't want to start an argument with a woman who's asking how she looks in an ugly dress.

"Well, that's a load of bullshit." I drop onto my bed across from where Drake stands in the middle of my room. We're close enough I can nudge him with my toes. "I'm sorry, man. I keep trying."

Of course I've been trying to summon his goddess. Every quiet moment, I send up a prayer asking her to help him. The man, the goose, the chair, he means a lot to me and I want to help him.

"You have?" There's surprise in his voice and I realize that he has no idea how much I've grown to appreciate him.

"Of course, Drake." I nudge him again and offer up a smile I don't really feel. "I'm not going to leave you hanging if I can do something."

"Why?"

10 DRAKE

was certain Evan hadn't done a thing since the first time he'd tried and failed to summon my goddess. My wonderful, stubborn goddess.

I've wondered if he was trying to keep me here. A part of me feared it. And a part of me hoped it. And all of me longed for him.

There's a part of me certain that the human feels this connection growing between us. This tug at my center that only calms when he's around. This simmer of desire that only flashes when he's near.

But he's been very careful around me. There has been no repeat of that first night when he'd rode me hard. He keeps his distance from me at all times. A chair without a use. A heart without a home.

The whole thing is ridiculous, of course. I'm a centuries old being who has seen it all. I've never wanted for companionship when I desired it. Never wanted for anything, really. Maybe that's why this want for Evan is so all-consuming.

"Because you matter. You don't deserve to be stuck like this." Evan waves a hand at me. I know he means my chair form but for a moment, I wish he meant more. I wish he knew how I felt so he could put an end to this agony of wanting.

And it is agony. Which is why I strike out, rather than endure the pain alone. "Yeah, the sooner I'm gone, the sooner you can get back to your normal life. Get laid before your dick falls off, isn't that what your roommate said before he left? We wouldn't want to lose your pretty penis."

The silence that follows my outburst is heavy. I have more than enough time to regret my words and an apology is on my metaphorical tongue when Evan finally speaks.

"Is that what you think?" His voice is calm, but frosty. His words would make the goddess of winter proud. "For someone who has lived so long, you're just as idiotic as the rest of them."

"What's that supposed to mean?" I stamp down the hope that's trying to swell inside of me. Being called an idiot should not be making me feel hopeful, and yet.

And yet.

"I thought we were friends, you idiot." Evan pushes to his feet and stands in front of me with his hands on his hips. "You asked for my help. Of course I'm going to help you. If you don't want me to, just fucking say so."

"I don't know what I want!" The words burst free of me and startle us both. "Being stuck like this is Hell. Being free would mean returning to my post. Being free would mean leaving you."

"Don't make this about me." But he takes a small step forward until his dark grey sweatpants brush against the front of my seat. "I'll be alright."

"What if I won't be?"

11 EVAN

My heart races at Drake's words and the meaning behind them. At the implication that he wants to be here as much as I want him here.

It's an impossible future. He's a fucking chair and there's no sign of his goddess. But that doesn't feel important.

"I've fucked my way through centuries, but I've never wanted anyone the way I want you." The words sounded forced, broken. And in that moment, I know he feels the impossibility of it. But maybe, maybe he doesn't care.

I fall to my knees and grip the arms. The fabric is soft and warm under my hands and Drake's woodsy scent floods my senses.

"I don't know what we're doing," I say, stroking along the arms and up the sides. "This is insane."

"I've done weirder." I freeze and stare at him, raising my eyebrows. He lets out a laugh. "Okay, maybe not. I just don't want you to stop."

"Does it feel good?" I run my hands back down the sides of the wings and grip the arms again. "Tell me what feels good."

Drake groans when I trail my fingers gently along the back and press them against the seam where the seat cushion meets the frame. I have no clue what I'm doing. I just know I want to make him feel good.

"You, touching me. All of it feels good when your hands are on me." Drake says.

So I touch him. I close my eyes and rub my hands down the cushion to the base and enjoy the feel of the velvety fabric beneath my hands. I grab the wooden legs and squeeze before sliding my grip up and down like I would on my own dick.

Drake makes a strangled sound when I slide my fingers along the front edge, just under the cushion. So I do it again. He lets out a small whimper that has my cock rising to full attention. I love the sound of a man breaking.

"Fuck Evan," Drake pants. The chair sags against me as I continue to play with the crease beneath the seat at the same time I grip the arm. "More. Please."

I drop my head to the seat and grip the cushion as I finger the crease. As Drake continues to pant and whine, I wonder what it feels like to him. I try to translate the location and sensation to a human body but I can't. I want to ask, but I don't want to stop and make him think.

I just want him to feel.

When I slide my whole hand under the cushion, the chair begins to shake underneath me. My cock is so hard it's almost painful. I want to wrap my hand around it but I also don't want to stop touching Drake.

I pull my hand free and he whines. The sound shudders through me. I want so many things in that moment and I can't have any of them.

My body craves contact. If he were human, I'd

be sucking his cock by now. Wrapping my tongue around the soft, hard flesh. If he were human, I'd want his hands in my hair, on my shoulders.

But he's not human and it's up to me to find pleasure for both of us.

12 DRAKE

'm tight as a bow as Evan slides his hand out from below my cushion and I can't help but let out a whine. It's not a sound I've made before but I don't have it in me to be embarrassed. It's just all too much.

What he's doing to me isn't like sex in my other forms. It's not as straight-forward as a touch to my cock or a deep press into my hole. It's more. It's like each touch is setting my every nerve ending on fire. It's pleasure unlike anything I've ever known.

Pure. Intense. Overwhelming.

"Please," I beg, unashamed of my need. I don't know how it will work but I can feel myself building up toward something. A release I don't understand. An orgasm I won't be denied.

"What do you want?" Evan says, trailing lazy fingers along my cushion. Sensation shudders through me. "What do you need?"

"You. More. I don't know." My entire frame shakes as Evan slides his hand down my leg. "I want you to fuck me."

I regret the words immediately. Of course he can't fuck me. I'm a godsdamn chair. I don't have a cock for him to suck or ride. I don't have a wet hole for him to sink into. I'm wood and springs and feathers.

"How?" Evan asks as his hands still and return to gripping my arms. "How would it make you feel good?"

His hands slide up my arms and I groan. "Do you want me to ride your arm like I did that first night? The smell of you, it does something to me."

He drops his head forward until his face is pressed to the cushion and he can breathe deep. I shudder when his hands grip me harder.

"That was nice," I gasp out around the unbelievable pressure in my chest.

Evan picks up his head as his hands slide down the front of my arms and he leans back until he can trace against the seam between my cushion and the base. I go rigid as he teases a finger beneath. It's like he's wrapping a hand around my cock and sliding deep at the same time.

"Or I can just tease you here." Evan's voice is gravel as he does just that. It's so good.

But it's not enough. I need more from him. I need him deep. And I need him as undone as I am. I growl in frustration and rock toward him, needing to do more. To make him as crazy as I feel.

"I need you," I tell him, not entirely sure what I'm asking.

"I've got you," Evan promises, sliding his hand flat beneath the cushion. "I'll make you feel so good."

"I want to make you feel good," I growl, frustrated. "Ride me, fuck me, get yourself off on me."

There's a pause and I think I've asked for too much, pushed him too far out of his comfort zone. I'm a chair for fuck's sake. What do can I possibly expect from him?

But then he rises up to his knees and shoves his sweatpants down over his thighs. I flash hot as his hard cock springs free. I don't care where he puts it, but I want it on me. Now.

13 EVAN

can't believe I'm about to do this.

My pants get tangled on my knees so I stand up and shove them all the way down before kicking them off. My dick is so hard it aches. I can't stop myself from grabbing it and giving it two short, hard pumps.

"Tease," Drake accuses with a half laugh, half groan.

"I would never," I gasp, faux insulted. I punctuate it with another pump of my cock before I fall back to my knees before him.

I glide my hands over the cushions, trying to prepare myself for what I'm about to do. I'm not exactly vanilla but I can't say I've ever put my cock anywhere it wasn't supposed to go before. This feels dirtier than any sex I've had in my life.

"Please, Evan. Fuck me." I flash hot at the plea. At the sound of this ancient being begging for me. It's heady.

Drake's begging makes it easy to do what comes next. I position myself on my knees until I can run the head of my cock along the seam between the cushion and the frame that seems to drive him crazy.

Precum darkens the purple fabric as I tease both of us. Finally, I angle the head of my cock until I can slide it beneath the cushion.

"Fuck," Drake pants out. The chair is shaking so hard I don't even have to move. It rocks into me as I thrust forward until my entire dick is buried in the cushion.

There are no words to describe the feel. It's nothing like fucking, but it's still so good. The soft velvety feel of the cushion surrounds the top of my cock in a soft slide. The coarser fabric of the frame drags along the bottom. The weight of the seat versus the stiffness of the frame work together to add battling sensations that shudder through my entire body.

It's weird. So fucking weird. But the way Drake is shaking and moaning and cursing has my balls drawing tight within a few thrusts. It shouldn't feel this good. It shouldn't be getting me off. But I can't deny that I'm close to coming.

Drake is rocking back and forth, taking my cock deep into his seat. I grip his arms and help move him back and forth down my length.

"Fuck, so good." He says, pressed against me. "Tell me it feels good. Tell me this is doing something for you. I need you to come for me."

The need in his voice does more for me than the friction of his movements. The desperation for my pleasure has me rocketing right to the edge as electricity shoots down my spine and gathers low.

"Fuck Drake, I'm going to come." I warn him. I try to pull out as I feel the start of my orgasm hit but he slams against my body and follows me as I try to retreat. I have no choice but to shoot my load underneath his cushion.

"Yes," Drake moans, shuddering to a stop

against me. There's a tearing sound and feathers explode out of the cushion in a puff. "Oh, fuck."

I jerk back, worried he's hurt himself. But other than a small rip in the seam, there's nothing.

"Well, I didn't expect that," Drake says with a breathless laugh.

"Neither did I," says a feminine voice from across the room.

14 DRAKE

Evan scrambles to his feet and pulls the comforter off of his bed to cover himself. I feel a profound sense of loss as he pulls free from me. My body still humming from the orgasm I'd just had but the afterglow is gone as soon as I register the being that interrupted us.

"You have terrible timing," I tell the goddess standing near the windows. She tips her lips up but the smile doesn't reach her eyes.

"I've been looking for you," Her voice is sweet. Everything about Brigid is sweet from her long red waves to the soft pink dress. "You've been missed, friend."

Evan makes a small sound in his throat. My focus switches back to him as he wraps the blanket around his hips. His face is still flushed but there's a tension in his jaw and between his eyes. Not the panic of a moment ago from being caught. It's something else.

Brigid doesn't acknowledge him. Her focus is fully on me. For some reason, the slight bothers me.

"It's time to go home," Brigid says, reaching a hand out to me.

"He is home," Evan props his fists on his hips and glares at the goddess. My heart swells even as fear chokes me. Brigid isn't prone to temper as some deities are, but it's never wise for a mortal to challenge a goddess.

"I've been telling you where he is for over a week. You just now decided to come get him? You haven't been looking for him. You haven't missed him." Evan's chest is heaving as he spits the words at Brigid. My own chest is tight as I wait for the response.

"Don't go," Evan turns to me with wide eyes. "Stay. Stay with me."

It's an impossible request. One he can't understand. But oh, how I want to. I lean toward him, wanting to touch him. Fuck, I want to hold him. Kiss him. Spend all of time with him.

"He can't," Brigid says, finally acknowledging Evan's existence. "Drake needs to come with me now."

Her voice is kind but there's steel behind it. As much as I wish things were different, I know she's right. Celestial beings cannot exist long on the human plane. And immortals falling for humans brings nothing but pain. I know this to be true, but I ache at the loss I know is coming.

Evan drops to his knees and grips my arms. His focus is intent on me, heedless of the goddess in the room. "Stay."

"I can't," I tell him, ripping out my heart to leave behind. "I have to return. We always knew this was coming."

I tilt forward until I can rest against him. I soak in his warmth and the way it feels to know for this moment at least, he's mine.

My focus shifts to Brigid and she nods. I can read the sympathy in her gaze and cannot stand it.

"Thank you," I tell Evan, pressing hard against him.

He opens his mouth to say something but before I can hear it, Brigid reaches a hand out to grip my back and, in the blink of an eye, we're gone.

15 EVAN

"We're going out tonight," Dave says, watching me from across the kitchen island as I make toast and coffee. "You've got to get out of this house."

"Pass," I say, dropping my knife into the sink before grabbing my plate and mug. "I'm busy."

"Evan," Dave's voice is gentle and I don't want to hear it. "I'm not going to force you to tell me what's wrong but I know you well enough to know something isn't right. You can't spend forever hiding from whatever it is in your bedroom."

"I'm not hiding." I tell him as I leave the kitchen, and him, behind.

I know he's worried about me. He's been trying to talk me into going out for weeks now, but I'm not interested. He'd even called our old roommate Jake over to try to lure me out. It only made things worse. Why did Jake get to be with the man he loved and I couldn't?

Three weeks. Three weeks since Drake left me and I still am not okay. I'd thought maybe once I couldn't smell him every day, I'd get over it. But the loss of his scent only broke my heart more.

Anger fought against pain inside me as I climbed the stairs. Anger at myself for being dumb enough to fall in love in a week. Anger at Drake for not even trying to fight for us. Anger at his goddess for being an unfeeling bitch. Anger at the universe for putting him in my life only to snatch him away.

I slam into my room and drop my toast and coffee on the desk, no longer interested in it. I drop back onto my bed and fist the blankets in my hands as I stare at the ceiling. My eyes close and I swallow back the anger and the tears behind it.

"Fuck you," I growl, tired of it all.

"I mean, I wouldn't say no." The deep voice comes from the direction of my desk. "But we should probably talk first."

My eyes fly open and I'm moving before I even register the action. The man leaning against my desk, sipping my coffee is a stranger. He's over six feet tall with curling blond hair and golden brown eyes. His broad body is dressed casually in a pair of grey sweatpants and a black t-shirt.

I'd recognize him anywhere.

"Drake," I say, surging to my feet. "How?"

I stop just short of touching him. My fingers tingle with the need to reach out and make sure he's real but I'm afraid of what I'll do when I make contact. My heart is racing in my chest and I feel like all the air was sucked out of the room.

Him being here is an impossible wish but I'm afraid of it. If he tells me he's not staying, I don't know how I'll survive the loss of him again.

"There are some perks to being an immortal being with connections to the gods." He flexes his fingers and sets the coffee mug back on the desk. "For example, they restored my forms, which took time."

His gaze is intent on me and I can feel it like a

physical touch. I close my eyes as I fight the need to throw myself on him.

"Then I had to convince a couple of stubborn gods to help me. Called in a few favors. A little minor blackmail. But it doesn't matter, because I'm here now. So long as you still want me."

There is vulnerability in those golden eyes. Tension in his body as he waits for my response. A fear I understand all too well.

Without a word, I close the gap between us and reach a hand up to wrap around the back of his neck. I pull him down to me and close the distance until our lips can brush.

The kiss explodes in sparks between us. All of the pain from the last week blooms into need. Drake is clearly feeling it too because his hands drive into my hair as he drags me closer. His tongue demands entry.

I open on a whimper. I release his neck and slide my hands down his arms and around his back until his entire body is flush against mine and it still isn't enough.

"More," I demand against Drake's mouth, unwilling to break that contact even as I slide my hands under his shirt, seeking the warmth of his skin.

"Evan," his voice comes out a moan. He breaks contact long enough to haul his shirt over his head and then he's back against me. His mouth pressing firmly against my mouth, devouring me.

It's still not enough. I need more. I pull back enough to lose my own shirt before bringing him back against me, skin to skin. His hands move to my waist and his callused grip digs into my sides.

"I've missed you," Drake's voice is broken, his eyes haunted. "I need you."

The words shoot through me as he gives words

to the feelings inside of me. Want and need and joy battle inside of me as I press kisses along his shoulder.

"I'm right here," I say against his skin. "Take what you need."

16 DRAKE

Evan drops to his knees in front of me and nuzzles his cheek against my straining cock and I almost come on the spot. I want this so bad. My need for him is a physical ache through my body.

My body. I flex my fingers and revel in the sensation of it. It's more than being back in my human form. It's everything. All the things I still have to tell Evan.

All things that fly out of my head when Evan tugs the waistband of my pants down to expose my cock. It's painfully hard and already leaking for him.

"And you called my cock pretty," Evan says just before he leans forward to lick a broad stripe over the head, lapping up the precum beaded there.

"Prettiest I've seen," I pant out as Evan's tongue continues to lick me. My hands flex at my sides as I fight the urge to tangle them in his hair and direct his mouth down my length. I don't want to rush this, but I'm already so close to coming.

I throw my head back when he finally takes me into his mouth and sucks. I can't stop myself from tangling my fingers in his dark strands. I can't stop the small thrusts of my hips as he works his mouth over me.

"Fuck, yes, fuck," I pant, forcing myself to remain as still as possible so I don't hurt him. Evan wraps a hand around my base and squeezes tight.

"Fuck me," Evan says, coming off my cock. A trail of saliva running from his lip to my tip. His tongue darts out to lick it up as he gazes up at me. "You don't have to be gentle. I can take it."

Before I can tell him I don't want to be rough with him, he's got the head of my cock back in his mouth and is sucking like he's trying to draw my soul out. There's no stopping myself from using my grip in his hair to drag him further down. My hips jerk forward until I can feel the tightness of his throat and hear him choke.

I pull back but he reaches up and grabs my ass, pulling me back against him in clear demand. I am helpless to disobey.

It doesn't take long. I'm too needy for him. It's just a matter of thrusts until I drive my length into his throat and I unload into his mouth. He keeps working me through my orgasm until my legs shake and I slump back onto the desk behind me.

Only then does Evan slide off my cock. He kisses the tip softly before looking up at me with a grin. His eyes are bright and watery, his mouth swollen and soft. I trace my thumb along his bottom lip, feeling lighter than I have in my entire long life.

When he wraps his hand around his cock, guilt hits me and I fall to my knees next to him.

"Thank you," I tell him, pressing my lips to his in a gentle caress. I reach out and wrap my hand around his cock, shoving his out of the way. It's wet with his precum, warm, hard.

I want to worship it. I want to feel it inside of

me. I want so many things but we have time. So I focus on jerking him off as I devour his mouth.

One of his hand is tangled in my hair and the other is gripping my shoulders as he thrusts into my hand. His sweet little whimpers as he gets close has my cock stirring to life again.

"Be a good boy and come for me," I say against his swollen mouth as I drag my hand up his cock, teasing his wet slit with my thumb.

That's all it takes. He explodes over my hand, cum coats my stomach in hot spurts. I continue to work his cock until the last drop. Evan slumps back on his heels.

My eyes are locked on his as I bring my hand up and lick the cum off. He tastes salty and hot. I cannot get enough. Especially when he groans and licks his lips.

17 EVAN

t takes a long while for us to get up and make our way to the shower. The tub, which always felt big enough, barely holds the two of us as we clean my cum off. Neither of us say much as we clean and dry off.

I'm afraid to say anything and break this warm afterglow. The goddess said Drake couldn't stay and he hasn't said he won't be leaving again. What just happened between us was so perfect I don't want to ruin it with hard truths.

"I'm going to have to go shopping," Drake says, tugging his sweatpants on. "My shirt got cum on it."

He holds up the black garment to show me the white spots. "Oops?"

Of course I'm not sorry. His body is a wonder. Broad and hard, a matte of hair over his chest and slightly rounded belly. He was my every lumberjack fantasy in real life.

"Brat," he throws the shirt at me. I catch it and toss it toward the bathroom where the hamper lives. I'd offer him one of mine but there's no way it will fit. I'm not a small man but Drake has inches on me in both height and breadth.

I tug my own pants on and reach for a shirt but Drake pulls it out of my hand and tosses it away. "If I have to be half naked, so do you."

"It's only fair." I agree. Drake pulls me toward the bed and we climb in, wrapping up in each other.

Comfort and warmth seep into me as we lay there in silence but it can't last.

"When do you leave?" I ask, bracing myself for the hurt.

"Leave?" Drake's deep voice is confused.

"You said you couldn't stay."

"That was before." Drake turns to his side to face me. He props himself up on one arm and reaches out to trace a finger down the side of my face. "Those favors I called in? It was to make it possible for me to stay. An immortal being might not be able to stay on the human plane, but there are ways to change that."

"I don't understand." I grip his hand in mine and pull it to my chest. My heart is racing as hope blooms inside of me. "You're staying?"

"I can't go back." Drake squeezes my fingers. "I'm as human as you are now."

"How?" It doesn't feel real and yet joy is beating at the inside of my chest.

"Does it matter?" He leans forward and gives me a gentle kiss. He pulls back with a frown. "Unless you don't want me to stay. I can't go back but you don't have to keep me. I just, I wanted, I—"

I wrap my free hand around the back of Drake's neck and force his gaze to mine. "I love you. I'm not letting you go. Not ever again."

"Thank gods."

Drake's mouth meets mine again and it's the only thing that matters.

ABOUT THE AUTHOR

Sabrina Cross (she/her) is a neurospicy 80's baby from the middle of nowhere Michigan, where she still lives with her cat. She came into her monster romance era early when she fell in love with Beast from the 1997's X-Men animated series. After discovering sentient object romance in early 2023, Sabrina decided to embrace what she calls her 'Hold My Beer' style of writing and gave into the lifelong dream of being an author. When not writing weird monster/sentient object smut, Sabrina can be found hanging out on social media (@authorsabrinacross), reading, or hoarding office supplies.

ALSO BY SABRINA CROSS

Yarn & Monsters Series

A True Love Spell Gone Wrong...

When four friends perform a true love spell, things go terribly wrong. Now they're locked into a deal with the devil and have only a year to find love and happiness or their souls are destined to face the flames. Armed with a demon guardian; Clover, Jasmine, Fern, and Violet are determined to beat the devil and save themselves. Except, this curse might be the best thing that's ever happened to them.

Corny: A F/F Candy Corn Romance

Snuggle: A M/F Demon Teddy Bear Romance

Tangled: A M/F Friends-To-Lovers Sentient Object Romance

Knotted: A M/F Demon Werewolf Romance

The Cursed Matchmaker Series

Never Piss off a witch. Or else you may find yourself trapped in a glory hole booth at an upscale sex club. But when the perfect couples hook up anonymously, Josh has no choice but to speak out and help them find love.

The Glory Whole Package

The Glory Whole Experiment

The Glory Whole Redemption

Retro Whimsy Series

Welcome to Retro Whimsy where nothing is as it seems and the owners know just what you need.

Getting Railed

Trogg Trouble

Game Girl

Retro Whimsy Series

Welcome to Retro Whimsy where nothing is as it seems
and the owners know just what you need.

Light Me Up

Sit Me Down

Ghostlight Falls - Shared World Series

Cooking Up A Demon

Planet WLN269 Needs Women - Shared World Series

Taken in by the Aliens

Much Ado About Rutting

Stand Alone Monster Romance

Christmas with the Monster

Can't Yeti Enough

Stand Alone Sentient Object Romance

Pounded by the Pommel Horse

Sentient Pen15 from Outer Space

Knotty Broomsticks